A Squash and a Squeeze

In memory of our first editor, Elke Lacey,
and for her son, Fred.

First published 1993 by Methuen Children's Books
First published 2003 by Macmillan Children's Books
This edition published 2014 by Macmillan Children's Books
a division of Macmillan Publishers Limited
20 New Wharf Road, London N1 9RR
Basingstoke and Oxford
Associated companies throughout the world
www.panmacmillan.com

ISBN: 978-1-4472-8225-9

Text copyright © Julia Donaldson 1993
Illustrations copyright © Axel Scheffler 1993 and 2003
Moral rights asserted

2 4 6 8 9 7 5 3 1

A CIP catalogue record for this book is available from the British Library.

Printed in China

A Squash and a Squeeze

Julia Donaldson
Illustrated by Axel Scheffler

MACMILLAN CHILDREN'S BOOKS

A little old lady lived all by herself
With a table and chairs and a jug on the shelf.

A wise old man heard her grumble and grouse,
"There's not enough room in my house.
Wise old man, won't you help me, please?
My house is a squash and a squeeze."

"Take in your hen," said the wise old man.

"Take in my hen? What a curious plan."

Well, the hen laid an egg on the fireside rug,

And flapped round the room knocking over the jug.

The little old lady cried, "What shall I do?
It was poky for one and it's tiny for two.
My nose has a tickle and there's no room to sneeze.
My house is a squash and a squeeze."

And she said, "Wise old man,
        won't you help me, please?
My house is a squash and a squeeze."

"Take in your goat," said the wise old man.

"Take in my goat? What a curious plan."

Well, the goat chewed the curtains
and trod on the egg,

Then sat down to nibble the table leg.

The little old lady cried, "Glory be!
It was tiny for two and it's titchy for three.
The hen pecks the goat and the goat's got fleas.
My house is a squash and a squeeze."

And she said, "Wise old man,
        won't you help me please?
My house is a squash and a squeeze."

"Take in your pig," said the wise old man.

"Take in my pig? What a curious plan."

So she took in her pig who kept chasing the hen,

And raiding the larder again and again.

The little old lady cried, "Stop, I implore!
It was titchy for three and it's teeny for four.
Even the pig in the larder agrees,
My house is a squash and a squeeze."

And she said, "Wise old man,
        won't you help me please?
My house is a squash and a squeeze."

"Take in your cow," said the wise old man.

"Take in my cow? What a curious plan."

Well, the cow took one look
    and charged straight at the pig,
Then jumped on the table and tapped out a jig.

The little old lady cried, "Heavens alive!
It was teeny for four and it's weeny for five.
I'm tearing my hair out, I'm down on my knees.
My house is a squash and a squeeze."

And she said, "Wise old man,
        won't you help me please?
My house is a squash and a squeeze."

"Take them all out," said the wise old man.
"But then I'll be back where I first began."

So she opened the window and out flew the hen.
"That's better — at last I can sneeze again."

She shooed out the goat and she shoved out the pig.
"My house is beginning to feel pretty big."

She huffed and she puffed
and she pushed out the cow.
"Just look at my house, it's enormous now.

"Thank you, old man, for the work you have done.
It was weeny for five, it's gigantic for one.
There's no need to grumble
     and there's no need to grouse.
There's plenty of room in my house."

And now she's full of frolics and fiddle-de-dees.
It isn't a squash and it isn't a squeeze.

Yes, she's full of frolics and fiddle-de-dees.
It isn't a squash and a squeeze.

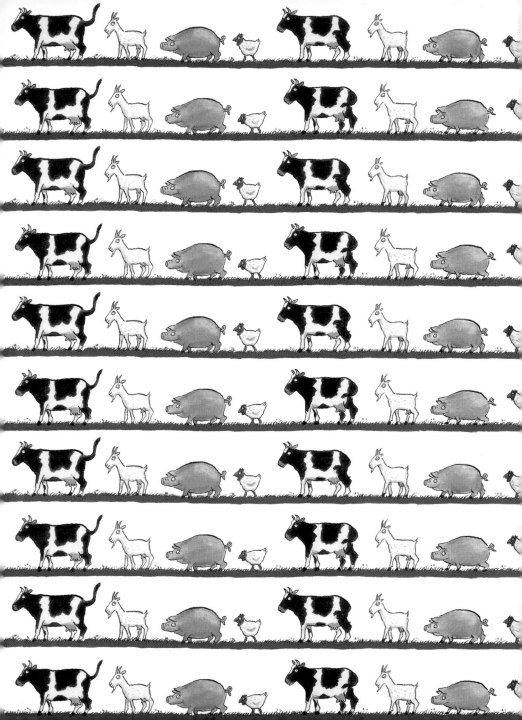

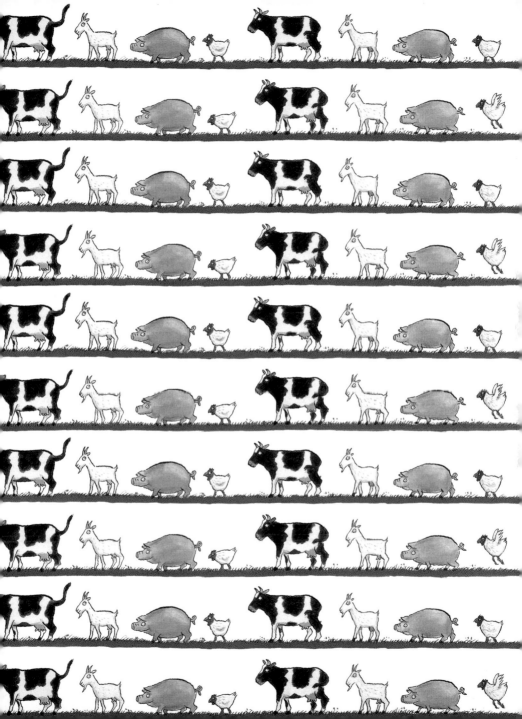